# BEGINNER READER

## RAINBOW magic™

# The Pet Keeper Fairies

Orchard Beginner Readers are specially created to develop literacy skills, confidence and a love of reading.

ORCHARD BOOKS
First published in the USA in 2013 by Scholastic Inc
First published in Great Britain in 2017 by The Watts Publishing Group
This edition published in 2018 by The Watts Publishing Group

5 7 9 10 8 6 4

Copyright © 2018 Rainbow Magic Limited.
Copyright © 2018 HIT Entertainment Limited.
Illustrations copyright © Orchard Books 2017

HiT entertainment

A CIP catalogue record for this book is available from the British Library.

ISBN 978 1 40833 976 3

Printed in China

FSC
www.fsc.org

MIX
Paper from
responsible sources
FSC® C104740

The paper and board used in this book are made from wood from responsible sources
Orchard Books
An imprint of Hachette Children's Group
Part of The Watts Publishing Group Limited
Carmelite House, 50 Victoria Embankment, London EC4Y 0DZ

An Hachette UK Company
www.hachette.co.uk
www.hachettechildrens.co.uk

# BEGINNER READER

# RAINBOW
## magic™

# The Pet Keeper
# Fairies

Daisy Meadows

ORCHARD

Spring has sprung!
The Pet Fairies and their pets are thrilled.

The weather is beautiful and there is so much to do!

Bella cleans her bunny's pen.
Molly and Harriet hang up the washing.

Penny washes her pony's winter blanket.
"It's too warm for a blanket now!" she says.

Georgia, Katie and Lauren have finished their chores. They want to ride in the royal hot air balloon.

"It's the perfect day for it," Lauren says.

Georgia sees something coming over the hill.
"It's Sparky, my guinea pig!" she says.
"Shimmer the kitten and Sunny the puppy
are with him."

"Where have you all been?" Katie asks.
Sparky squeaks and runs in circles.
Sunny jumps.
Shimmer points.

"You are so silly," Georgia says with a laugh.
The hot air balloon lands in the field.
"It's our turn," Katie says.

Suddenly, Sparky jumps up.
He grabs Georgia's wand in his teeth.

"Sparky!" Georgia yells.
The guinea pig takes off over the hill.

The puppy and kitten follow behind him.
"Our animals are trying to tell us something,"
Georgia says. "They must need our help."

The three fairies fly after their animals.
"Look, they're going into the Fairyland
Palace," Katie says.

Sparky disappears through a tiny doorway.
"The door is so small," Lauren says worriedly.
"We should follow them," Katie says.

Katie waves her wand, and the three
fairies shrink.
"Now we will fit," Katie declares.

They all scamper through the small door.
"Whoever lives here must be really tiny,"
Lauren says.

"Look – there's Sparky," Georgia says.
Sparky waves his paw.

The fairies follow Sparky into a courtyard.
A family of mice is there.
They are all looking up.
The fairies join them.

"Oh, no!" Lauren cries.
Far above, there is a tiny, scared mouse.
He is on a high branch of a tall lilac tree.

"Miles climbed up," says the mummy mouse.
"He can't get down."

"We can help," Georgia says.
She nods to Sparky.
The guinea pig gives Georgia her wand.
Georgia recites a spell.

"With a fire for heat, the air will rise
And carry you back down from the skies.
But don't you fret or float away.
Return to safe ground, please don't delay."

There is a burst of sparkles,
and a hot air balloon appears.
It rises up to the tree.

Miles hops inside and the balloon drifts down.

Miles looks over the edge of the basket
and he jumps.
The tiny mouse lands safely and runs into
his mother's arms.
"Oh, thank you!" the daddy mouse exclaims.

The family gives Miles a big hug.
"We should all thank Sparky, Shimmer and Sunny," Georgia says.
She gives her guinea pig a good pat.

The fairies say goodbye to the mouse family.
As they leave the palace, Sparky steals
Georgia's wand again.

"Where's he going now?" Georgia wonders.
The fairies chase Sparky over a hill.

Sparky has climbed into the balloon!
"Follow Sparky, everyone!" Georgia calls.
"It's our turn for a balloon ride!"